Chelsea
the
Congratulations
Fairy

Special thanks to Shannon Penney

No part of this publication may be reproduced, stored in a retrieval system, or transmitted in any form or by any means, electronic, mechanical, photocopying, recording, or otherwise, without written permission of the publisher. For information regarding permission, write to Rainbow Magic Limited, c/o HIT Entertainment, 830 South Greenville Avenue, Allen, TX 75002-3320.

ISBN 978-0-545-70826-5

12 11 10 9 8 7 6 5 4 3 2 1   15 16 17 18 19 20/0

Printed in the U.S.A.   40

First printing, May 2015

Chelsea

the
Congratulations
Fairy

by Daisy Meadows

SCHOLASTIC INC.

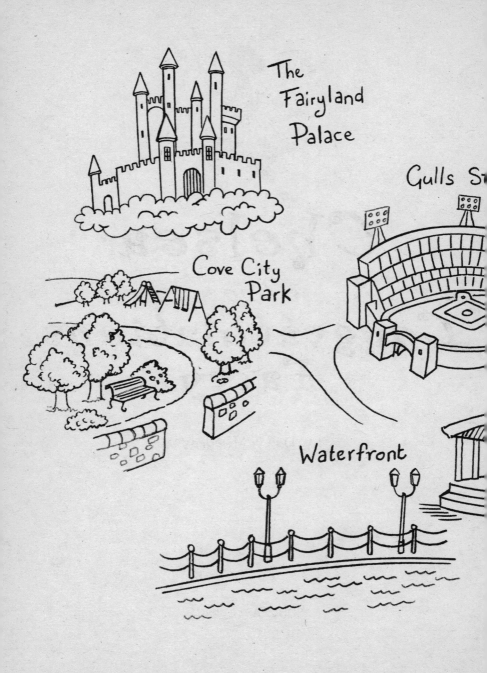

The
Fairyland
Palace

Gulls St

Cove City
Park

Waterfront

dium

Jack Frost's
Ice Castle

Cove City
Zoo

Bandshell

ZOO

I'm sick and tired of sweet celebrations
For milestones, achievements, and graduations.
I'm putting a stop to all this fun—
Thanks to me, Jack Frost, it's finally done!

The magic tulip, balloon, and diploma, too,
Are mine, pesky fairies! And there's nothing you can do.
I'll hide them away, far out of sight.
Congrats to me—now things are just right!

**Find the hidden letters in the balloons
throughout this book. Unscramble all 8 letters
to spell a special congratulations word!**

First-Pitch Fears

Contents

A Surprising Snack

"I'm so excited to go to a real professional baseball game, Kirsty!" Rachel Walker said, squeezing her best friend's hand. Together, they stepped off the city bus outside the stadium.

"Me, too!" Kirsty Tate said with a little skip. "Thanks so much for inviting me along this weekend. Cove City is the best!"

Rachel grinned. Kirsty was right—Cove City was one of her very favorite places to visit. Luckily, her cousin Ivy's family lived in the city, so Rachel and her parents came to see them often. But this weekend, they were here for a very special occasion: Ivy's high school graduation! There were lots of activities planned, and the girls couldn't wait to see and do as much as possible during their trip. They

due

...ways had magical adventures when ...y were together!

...irsty and Rachel stopped to look ...und inside the stadium's enormous ...ryway. Everything was decorated in ...e and white, the colors of the Cove ...y Gulls baseball team. There were ...d carts, gift shops, trophy cases, and ...ners celebrating the team as far as ...eye could see.

omen enjoye...
herokees orig...
...a, northern G...
...y were surpris...
...he Cherokees...
...n his mother's...
...s mother, and...
...r), his mother...
...er. The most i...
...how this kins...
...t the Cheroke...
...control over t...

...n were the hea...
...generations (g...
...umber of diffe...
...walls and a ro...
...cribs and sto...
...from their m...
...nd wife did n...
...ained with th...

...uses and cul...

"Come on, you two!" Ivy called from up ahead, with the rest of her cousins close behind. "The field is this way!"

The girls ran to catch up to the group. "It's so cool that we get to come early to watch batting practice and meet the players," Kirsty said breathlessly.

Ivy's eyes sparkled. "I'm a huge Gulls fan," she said, "so this is the perfect way to celebrate this special weekend—here, with all of you!" She gave Rachel's and Kirsty's shoulders a squeeze.

Ivy led the group down a long hallway. As they stepped

out into the sunshine, rows of seats and the wide, green baseball field stretched out before them. Rachel and Kirsty had never seen anything like it!

"I had no idea the field was so big!" Rachel exclaimed.

Kirsty nodded in wonder. "It's hard to tell when you're watching the game on TV."

The girls followed Ivy and the rest of Rachel's cousins down to a row of blue and white seats right behind home plate.

"Settle in,
everyone!"
Ivy said
with a
big smile.
"First, the
team takes
batting
practice,
and then we'll
get a chance to go onto the field."

Rachel shivered with excitement at the
thought of it.

Someone dressed as Sully, the team's
seagull mascot, came around to hand out
popcorn, peanuts, and boxes of Cracker
Jack. The group cheered wildly as the
Gulls took the field. Their starting

pitcher, Jim Fay, warmed up in the bullpen while other players stepped up to the plate to practice hitting.

"This is already such a great day—and it's barely even started," Rachel said to Kirsty, pulling open the top of her Cracker Jack box.

Before Kirsty could reply, the girls were hit with a rush of air and a puff of twinkling dust.

"What was that?" Kirsty cried.

Rachel looked down at her snack. "I think it came from my Cracker Jack box," she said in surprise. Then she lowered her voice, looking around to make sure none of her cousins overheard. "Kirsty, do you think that could have been . . . fairy dust?"

Kirsty's eyes grew wide. Both girls held

their breath as Rachel pulled back the flap of the box again.

Sure enough, nestled inside among the popcorn and peanuts was a tiny, sparkling fairy!

Batter Up!

"I'm so happy I found you!" the little fairy cried. Her dark hair was pulled into a side bun, and her purple dress stood out inside the Cracker Jack box. The girls had to lean in close to hear her. "I'm Chelsea the Congratulations Fairy—and I need your help!"

Rachel looked around to make sure

none of her cousins were
paying attention.
They were all too
busy watching
batting practice
to notice this
magical turn of
events! "It's nice
to meet you,
Chelsea," she
whispered with a smile.

"We're happy to help you," Kirsty
added, using her pinkie finger to shake
the little fairy's hand. "Let me guess—is
Jack Frost up to his old tricks again?"

Chelsea's sweet face turned sour at the
mention of Jack Frost's name. "You'd
think he'd get tired of being such a
horrible troublemaker!" she huffed.

"What did he do this time?" Rachel asked.

Chelsea sighed, sinking back onto a piece of popcorn. "He stole my three magic objects right out from under my nose! When I woke up this morning, they were missing. He must have snuck into my toadstool house while I was sleeping!" Her eyes narrowed. "If I'd been awake, there's no way he would have gotten away with it."

The girls frowned. This really was a new low for Jack Frost!

"I searched all over Fairyland, but I think he had his goblins hide the objects in your world," Chelsea continued. "I don't even know where to start looking for them!"

Kirsty popped a piece of Cracker Jack in her mouth and chewed thoughtfully. "What do your objects look like, Chelsea?"

"They're a yellow tulip, a red balloon, and a diploma," Chelsea replied. Her face fell. "Together, they help people everywhere achieve accomplishments and take important steps from one thing to the next. My tulip controls courage, helping people be brave and try new things—even if they're scary. My balloon controls confidence, helping people believe in themselves and know that they can meet their goals. And my diploma controls persistence, helping people stick with things and see them through to the end."

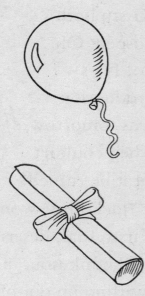

"Those sound really important," Rachel commented.

Chelsea flopped over dramatically. "Exactly! Without them, all sorts of accomplishments and milestones are going to turn into disasters— including graduations!"

Rachel and
Kirsty both
gasped. Oh,
no! Ivy's
graduation
was tomorrow.
They couldn't
let it be ruined!

"Jack Frost won't get away with this!"
Kirsty said, determined.

"Thank you, girls!" Chelsea cried,
twirling up out of the box to give them
each a peck on the cheek. She fluttered
down into Kirsty's shirt pocket. "I'll stay
here, out of sight, and do whatever I can
to help."

Just then, Ivy clapped her hands.
"Okay, everyone—batting practice is
over, which means it's our turn to go

take the field!" Her eyes glimmered as she led the group onto the field.

"Ivy is so excited about this weekend," Rachel whispered to Kirsty and Chelsea. "I don't want anything to spoil that."

As the girls stepped onto the huge field, they looked around in awe. This was amazing! Before they knew it, several of

the Gulls players had come up to shake their hands. They split the group in half, and one side played the field while the other took turns at bat.

For a little while, Rachel and Kirsty forgot all about Chelsea's magic objects. They were having too much fun! Ivy got a huge hit, and Rachel's cousin Sam made a few incredible catches in the outfield. Rachel and Kirsty both got hits, too. But running around the bases was exhausting—*whew!*

Rachel flopped down behind home plate to take a break, and Kirsty sat next to her, cross-legged. They cheered and clapped as others stepped up to bat.

After a few minutes, Kirsty nudged Rachel. "Look at that group of bat boys over there," she said, nodding toward the dugout. "Are they supposed to be goofing around like that?"

Rachel turned her gaze to where Kirsty was looking. She was surprised she hadn't noticed the boys before, since they were making so much noise.

"Hmm," Rachel muttered. Something about the boys seemed strange. "Chelsea, have you seen these boys before?" she whispered.

Chelsea peeked out of Kirsty's pocket, and the three friends watched the bat boys shoving, poking one another with bats, and tumbling in the dirt.

Suddenly, Rachel gasped. "Kirsty, I don't think those are bat boys," she said slowly, peering at their giant feet. "They're goblins!"

The Not-So-Lucky Winner

Kirsty's eyes grew wide. "You're right!" she cried. She could see the goblins' long green noses peeking out from under their baseball caps.

"We have to keep an eye on those goblins, girls," Chelsea said urgently, biting her lip. "I'm sure they'll lead us to one of my magic objects!"

Before Rachel and Kirsty could come up with a plan, the Gulls' star pitcher, Jim Fay, whistled for everyone to join him on the pitcher's mound.

"Great job, everyone!" he said as they gathered around. "Thanks for joining us today—and a very special congratulations to Ivy on her graduation tomorrow!" He gave Ivy a high five while everyone cheered.

"Before you head back to your seats," Jim continued, "I have a special surprise." He pulled off his baseball cap and held it out in front of him. "Anyone who wants to can write their name down and put it in my hat. I'll choose a name at random, and that person will get to throw the first pitch of the game today!"

The group buzzed with excitement. Rachel and Kirsty looked at each other in surprise. Wow!

Everyone wrote their names on little scraps of paper and tossed them into Jim's hat. The girls held their breath as he fished around in the hat and pulled out a name. Chelsea looked up out of Kirsty's pocket and grinned, crossing her fingers for good luck.

"And the lucky winner is . . . Kirsty!" Jim announced.

Kirsty clapped a hand over her mouth. She couldn't believe it!

The group cheered, and Rachel

and Ivy both gave her a big hug. When no one was looking, Chelsea even flashed a thumbs-up and shot a burst of

sparkly, celebratory
balloons from
her wand.

"Kirsty, you
and a friend
can stay
here, near
home plate,
until game
time," Jim told
her as the rest of
the group headed up
to their seats. "I'll be back soon for
your big moment!" He winked and
headed down the tunnel toward the
locker room.

"This is so exciting!" Rachel squealed,
squeezing Kirsty's hand.

Kirsty smiled, but didn't say anything.
She had been thrilled just a minute
ago . . . but now she suddenly had
butterflies in her stomach!

Rachel looked at her closely. "Kirsty,
what's wrong?"

"I'm scared!" Kirsty admitted with a

shrug. "Thousands of people will be watching. What if I do it wrong?"

Chelsea fluttered up out of Kirsty's pocket and settled on her shoulder. She tugged Kirsty's braid gently. "I think I know what's wrong. This is all because my magic tulip is missing!" She stomped her foot. "I wish I could give Jack Frost a piece of my mind right now."

Rachel leaned over so that she was eye level with the little fairy. "Your tulip controls courage, right?" she asked.

"Exactly," Chelsea said with a nod. "Without it, Kirsty, you aren't feeling very brave at all!"

Kirsty let out a big sigh. Chelsea was right about one thing—she was feeling less brave by the minute!

"We have to find the tulip before the game," Rachel said. She turned toward the dugout, where the rascally goblins were still goofing around, and raised an eyebrow. "Luckily, I know just where to start . . ."

Gotcha, Goblin!

Rachel, Kirsty, and Chelsea watched the goblins closely. They were climbing on top of the dugout and daring one another to jump onto the field.

"That looks dangerous," Kirsty whispered. "It's a long way down!"

Most of the goblins chickened out at the last minute and decided not to jump.

But one goblin leaped without hesitating for a second. He even did a flip in the air before landing firmly on his feet! The rest of the goblins whooped and cheered.

Chelsea drew in her breath slowly. "He's acting awfully brave . . . He must have my yellow tulip!"

The three friends peered at the brave goblin. Suddenly, Rachel nudged Kirsty and gasped.

"Look! In the buttonhole of his baseball jersey!" she said.

A bright yellow tulip was tucked in the goblin's buttonhole—and it was sparkling with fairy magic!

Chelsea zoomed into the air, flew a series of excited loops, and dove back into Kirsty's pocket before anyone could spot her. "That's it!" she cried in her tiny fairy voice.

Kirsty twirled her hair thoughtfully. "But how are we going to get it from him? It's right under his nose."

"I have an idea . . ." Rachel said with a grin. She leaned in to whisper the plan to her friends.

"Let's give it a try," Chelsea said, fluttering her wings anxiously inside Kirsty's pocket.

Kirsty giggled. "That tickles!"

Without a moment to waste, Rachel grabbed a baseball and Kirsty picked up a nearby bat.

"Ready?" Rachel called loudly, winding up to pitch. "Swing, batter batter batter!"

Kirsty swung wildly at the ball, but missed by a mile. She sighed dramatically. "Go again! I'll get it this time."

But each time Rachel pitched the ball, Kirsty swung and missed.

"Strike!" Rachel called, turn after turn.

Kirsty pretended to get frustrated. *"Ugh!"* she cried, kicking the dirt next to home plate. "I just can't seem to hit the

ball. I wish someone could show me what I'm doing wrong . . ."

As if on cue, the goblin with the yellow tulip dashed over from the dugout. "You're in luck!" he bragged. "I'm an amazing baseball player. I'll show you how it's done!"

With that, the goblin took Kirsty's bat and hit three pitches in a row. He really was a good player! Chelsea peeked up at Kirsty from inside her pocket, looking impressed.

"Wow," Kirsty said to the goblin. "You're the best baseball player I've ever met! Can you help me take a swing? I just know that I'll be able to do it if you're helping me."

The goblin smiled proudly, strutting around home plate and twirling the bat. "Of course, of course. I'm always happy to share my unbelievable talents."

Kirsty glanced down to see Chelsea roll her eyes. On the pitcher's mound, Rachel was trying to stifle a giggle. This goblin was awfully full of himself!

Kirsty made sure to stay on the goblin's good side. It was all part of the plan!

"Oh, thank you!" she said as the goblin stood behind her and helped her choke up on the bat.

"You see," the goblin began, "you just need to put your hands like this, and then when you see the ball coming, make sure you—"

But the goblin didn't have a chance to finish before Kirsty turned, plucked the magic tulip from his jersey, and quickly handed it to Chelsea. Immediately, the tulip shrunk to fairy-size! Chelsea fluttered high up into the air, out of reach, with a happy cheer.

The goblin froze, looking first at the trail of sparkling fairy dust in the air, and then down at his jersey. As he

realized what had
happened, his
mouth fell open.

"Horrible girls!
Pesky fairy!
You stole my
tulip!" he cried
indignantly,
throwing the bat
in anger.

Chelsea flew down to face
him, her hands on her hips. "Jack Frost
stole this tulip from *me*," she said firmly.
"You all really need to learn not to take
things that don't belong to you."

Before the goblin could stammer a
response, Chelsea blew each of the girls
a kiss, winked, and disappeared back to
Fairyland in the twinkling of an eye.

Magically Brave

The goblin stomped his feet and howled, "Get back here, you tricky fairy!"

But Chelsea was long gone.

From the dugout, the other goblins jeered at their friend.

"You let them take the tulip from right under your giant nose!" one cried.

"Jack Frost is going to be so mad at us!" called another.

The poor goblin looked like he didn't know what to say.

"Sorry about that," Kirsty said. "You are a great baseball player, though."

His green face lit up. "Really?" he asked hopefully.

"Absolutely," said Rachel, walking up to join them. "Maybe you could be on the Gulls one day!"

The goblin clapped his hands merrily at the thought.

Just then, the Gulls' manager called the bat boys away to get ready for the game. The goblin skipped off to join his friends.

The girls couldn't help laughing.

"Looks like it's almost game time," Rachel said, watching the stands fill with fans. "How are you feeling, Kirsty?"

Kirsty thought for a minute, then threw an arm around Rachel's shoulders. "Thanks to Chelsea and her magic tulip, I'm feeling braver than ever!"

"Are you ready, Kirsty?" Jim Fay

called, walking over. He handed her the game ball.

"I was born ready!" Kirsty replied.

With that, Jim led her out to a spot in front of the pitcher's mound. Kirsty waved and laughed as the announcer proclaimed for the whole stadium to hear: "Throwing today's first pitch is a very special guest of the Gulls, Miss Kirsty Tate!"

The crowd cheered wildly. Kirsty could
see Ivy and her cousins waving excitedly
from their seats.

She took a deep breath, kept her eye on
the catcher . . . and threw the ball right
into his mitt!

More cheers rang in her ears as she and
Jim jogged back to home plate together.

"You didn't seem nervous at all!"

Rachel cried, giving her a big hug.

"I wasn't," Kirsty said. "My nerves disappeared like . . . magic!"

Before the girls headed up to join Ivy and the group in their seats, Jim tapped Kirsty on the shoulder. He was holding a big bouquet of flowers.

"Congratulations on a great pitch," he said, giving her a high five and handing her the flowers.

Kirsty and Rachel thanked him and wished the team good luck as they

walked off the
field.

Suddenly,
Rachel
started
giggling.
"Kirsty, did
you take a close
look at your bouquet yet?"

Kirsty shook her head and looked
down at the flowers. They were all
bright yellow tulips!

She laughed, too. "I think Chelsea
would approve!"

Much Ado
at the Zoo

Contents

Animal Adventure

"I hope they have tigers!" Rachel said, linking arms with Kirsty and skipping down the city sidewalk. Cars, taxis, and buses zoomed down the busy street. Tall buildings towered all around.

Kirsty giggled. "And baboons!" She turned to smile at Rachel's parents, who strolled down the street behind the girls.

"Thanks so much for taking us to the Cove City Zoo this morning, Mr. and Mrs. Walker."

"It's nice to get out of the house and see the sights," Mrs. Walker replied.

"Besides, Ivy seemed awfully nervous about her graduation speech this afternoon," Mr. Walker added. Then he winked. "It's best that we stay out of her hair for a little while!"

Rachel raised an eyebrow at Kirsty. The girls knew that Ivy was feeling more than just regular nerves. "This is all because two of Chelsea the Congratulations Fairy's magic objects are still missing," she whispered.

"I know," Kirsty said with a sigh. She nudged Rachel with her elbow. "But cheer up! Maybe we'll find  one at the zoo. Look!"

Up ahead, the girls could see a huge iron gate topped with animal silhouettes. A colorful sign read *Welcome to the Cove City Zoo!* With a squeal, they both ran as fast as they could until they reached the gate.

"This is one of the biggest zoos in the country," Mrs. Walker said when she finally caught up.

Mr. Walker paid the admission fee and studied a map. "There's a lot to see," he said with a whistle. "You girls have your work cut out for you!"

Rachel grinned. "Can we explore on our own for a while?" she asked. Without her parents around, maybe she and Kirsty could find one of Chelsea's

magic objects . . . or maybe they'd even find Chelsea herself!

"Sure, I think that would be OK," Mrs. Walker said. "Why don't we meet in an hour by the penguin exhibit? They feed the penguins at eleven o'clock, and Ivy said we definitely shouldn't miss it." She circled it on the map.

"I love penguins!" Kirsty cried. "That sounds great."

Rachel gave
each of her
parents
a hug,
grabbed
Kirsty's hand,
and together
they ran off down the tree-lined path.

"The baboons are this way," Kirsty
said, pointing to the left.

Rachel pointed to the right. "And the

tigers are that way." Suddenly, she
stopped in her tracks. Just ahead, a
young woman in a green zookeeper
uniform sat alone on a bench. She held
her head in her hands. "Kirsty, look,"
Rachel whispered.

Kirsty peered at the woman. "She
looks awfully upset," she noted. "What
do you think could be wrong?"

"I don't know," Rachel said. "But
there's only one way to find out . . ."

Safari Magic

Rachel slowly approached the bench, with Kirsty close behind. She put a gentle hand on the zookeeper's shoulder. "Excuse me—are you OK?"

The young woman looked up in surprise. When she saw the girls' concerned faces, she gave them a small smile. "I'll be fine," she said. "Thanks for asking."

Kirsty noticed that the woman's name tag read CLARE. "You work here at the zoo, Clare?"

Clare sighed. "I'm new. Today is my first day in charge of the big penguin feeding."

"Oh!" Rachel's face lit up. "We're planning to watch that! I heard that it's a super-popular exhibit."

"It's many visitors' favorite part of the zoo," Clare said, looking even more worried than before. "And that makes my problem even worse! I've worked with these penguins a lot behind the scenes, and I have plenty of experience at other zoos, too. But in our  latest practice session, everything went wrong. The penguins wouldn't listen to me at all!"

Rachel and Kirsty looked at each other with raised eyebrows. Uh-oh! This must be because of Chelsea's missing magic objects . . .

Clare buried her head in her hands

again. "I'm sure that I'm going to disappoint all of the visitors who come to see the penguins today!"

"I wish there were something we could do to help you," Rachel said.

Kirsty squeezed Rachel's arm. "There is," she whispered. "We have to find Chelsea's magic objects—and fast!"

Rachel nodded, looking determined. "I hope everything goes better at the feeding, Clare," she said to the zookeeper. "We'll be cheering you on from the audience!"

"Good luck," Kirsty added. "You'll do great!"

Clare gave the girls a halfhearted smile and waved as they headed down the path.

"Poor Clare," Rachel said once they were out of earshot.

Kirsty sighed. "This is all Jack Frost's fault—and we're the only ones who can help. I just wish we knew where to look!"

Together, the girls headed into the area marked *Safari*. For a few minutes, they completely forgot about Chelsea's magic objects. Around every bend in the path they spotted roaring lions, trumpeting elephants, and towering giraffes!

"Wow!" Kirsty cried. "Those elephants were even bigger than I expected!"

"And look at that giraffe!" Rachel added, pointing. "I can barely see the top of its head behind that tall tree branch."

Kirsty squinted as the giraffe moved. "Doesn't the top of its head look a little . . . sparkly?" she asked slowly.

Rachel gasped. "It's Chelsea!"

Rachel was right! The tiny fairy was
perched on the giraffe's head, waving.
She fluttered down to see the girls,
leaving a trail of shimmering fairy dust
behind her. The giraffe nodded in a
friendly way and wandered off.

"Hi, girls!" Chelsea called, grinning as
she landed on Rachel's shoulder. "I was
hoping to find you here."

"We were hoping to find you, too," Kirsty said. "We've been searching for more of your magic objects, but we haven't had any luck yet."

The girls continued along the safari path, with Chelsea sitting comfortably on Rachel's shoulder.

"Things are going all wrong, Chelsea," Rachel said, looking glum. "My cousin Ivy is really nervous about her graduation speech, and we just met a zookeeper named Clare who's worried about disappointing fans at the penguin feeding."

Chelsea put her hands on her hips, suddenly looking spunky and determined. "This is all because my magic balloon is missing!" she cried. "It gives people confidence. We have to get it back!"

Something Fishy

The three friends made their way out of the safari exhibit and along another pathway, keeping their eyes open for anything magical. Colorful birds swooped overhead. A peacock even strutted right out in front of them!

Just then, Chelsea tugged on Rachel's ponytail. "One of my magic objects is nearby," she whispered excitedly. "I can sense it!"

Rachel and Kirsty peered all around, but they didn't see anything unusual. Kirsty peeked behind a shrub along the side of the path—and jumped when a frog hopped out and landed on her foot!

"The zoo is full of magical surprises," Kirsty said, laughing. "I just hope we can find the magic we're looking for!"

The girls continued toward the tiger exhibit. As they rounded a corner in the path, they spotted a huge cart rolling to a stop up ahead. Tied to the cart were tons and tons of balloons in all different colors!

"Wow," Rachel said. "Those are awfully pretty . . . but I thought balloons weren't allowed at the zoo."

Kirsty shook her head, suddenly looking angry. "They're not. If the

animals try to eat them, they could get really hurt!"

"I wonder what all of those balloons are doing here, then," Chelsea said, narrowing her eyes suspiciously. "Something fishy is going on!"

She darted behind a nearby tree, and the girls followed. They had a perfect view of the cart from their hiding spot! They could see three workers in zoo uniforms bustling around the cart, getting ready to open for the day. One pushed the cart, the second filled balloons from a helium tank, and the third was ready to deal with customers.

"Do you notice anything strange about those workers?" Kirsty asked.

Rachel squinted. "I can't see their faces because their hats are too low," she said. Then she gasped. "But they have gigantic *green* feet!"

"Goblins!" Chelsea cried, tumbling through the air in excitement. "And they have my magic balloon with them!"

Before the girls could say anything else, they were drowned out by the goblins, arguing loudly.

Chelsea rolled her eyes and sighed. "They're fighting. What else is new?" she muttered.

The girls listened closely.

"You were supposed to keep track of it!" one goblin cried, pointing at another.

That goblin shook his head. "No, no, no! It wasn't me. I'm in charge of collecting the money."

The third goblin held up his hands. "Don't look at me!" he said. "It's not my fault you lost it!"

The first goblin threw his hat to the ground in exasperation. "Jack Frost will never forgive us!"

Rachel's eyes widened. "Did they lose your magic balloon, Chelsea?"

Chelsea winked. "No, they just can't tell which one it is—it's mixed in with all of the other balloons!"

The girls stifled their giggles. The goblins were always causing extra trouble for themselves!

"I can tell which balloon is mine, though," Chelsea said. "Do you see that red one, in the middle of the bunch on the far left side?"

Kirsty and Rachel looked closely. "Oh, I see it now!" Kirsty whispered. "It's shimmering with a tiny bit of fairy magic!"

Chelsea nodded, her eyes twinkling. Then she frowned. "But how are we going to get it back? The goblins

may be foolish sometimes, but they surely won't let any of the balloons out of their sight."

"I have an idea," Kirsty said, looking thoughtful. She leaned in to whisper the plan to her friends, grinning. "It's crazy enough that it just might work!"

Up in the Air

With their plan in place, Rachel and Kirsty both took a deep breath. Chelsea was safely hidden behind Rachel's ponytail as the girls walked up to the balloon cart.

"Hi!" Rachel exclaimed, waving. The goblins stopped arguing and turned to scowl at her. "We'd like to buy forty balloons, please."

The goblins stared at them in shock. The girls could almost see the dollar signs shining in their greedy eyes.

"Excuse us for just one moment, ladies," one of them said politely, holding up a bony green finger.

The three goblins huddled together, muttering frantically. They were trying to be sneaky, but Rachel and Kirsty

could still hear snippets of their
conversation.

"We need to
make sure we
don't give them
the magic
balloon! Jack
Frost would be
really angry!"

"Just think of how much money we
could make, selling forty balloons at
once. Our first sale of the day! We'll
be rich!"

Rachel looked at Kirsty, nervous.
What would the goblins decide?

Finally, three green faces turned back
toward the girls. One of the goblins
cleared his throat. "We'd be very happy
to sell you forty balloons," he said.

Kirsty breathed a sigh of relief, and Rachel squeezed her arm. The goblins hadn't been able to resist making lots of money, just as the girls had hoped!

"Oh, thank you!" Kirsty said sweetly.

One goblin began carefully collecting forty balloons from the cart. He winced with the addition of each new balloon to the bunch. He was obviously worried about handing over the magic balloon by accident!

A tiny voice made Rachel's smile even wider. "My magic balloon is in the bunch now!" Chelsea whispered, tugging gently on Rachel's ponytail.

Rachel gave Kirsty a wink.

The goblin untied a few more balloons to add to the gigantic bunch in his hand. Suddenly . . . he was lifted up into the air! He was holding so many balloons that they carried him right up off the ground!

"HELP!" the goblin shrieked, kicking and flailing in midair. He clung to the balloon strings for dear life. "Help me!"

His goblin friends stared up at him in shock, frozen. By the time they made a move, the goblin with the balloons had floated too high. They couldn't reach him!

Just then, Chelsea sprang into action. She fluttered out from behind Rachel's ponytail and twirled up into the air, her party skirt floating around her.

"I'll make a deal with you!" she said cheerfully, hovering next to the panicking goblin.

His eyes were squeezed shut in fear, but they popped open when he heard Chelsea's voice. "Fairies!" he cried. "I should have known you pesky fairies were behind this trick!"

Chelsea put her hands on her hips and narrowed her eyes. "Would you like my help or not?"

The goblin looked down at the ground, which was getting farther and farther

away. "OK, OK!" he squealed. "What do you want?"

"It's simple," Chelsea said with a casual shrug. "You're holding my magic balloon. Just hand it over, and I'll get you down from there."

The goblin scowled. Below, his friends protested, jumping up and down and shaking their heads.

"Don't do it!" one cried.

"Jack Frost will be furious!" the other added with a shudder.

"Don't you think I know that?!" squealed the goblin in the air.

Kirsty looked at Rachel and crossed her fingers. They were so close to getting Chelsea's magic balloon back—but what if the goblin said *no*?

Balloon Bust

Chelsea zoomed around the goblin and the balloons, flying in a few dizzying loops. "Do we have a deal?" she asked.

The goblin glanced down at her—and squealed again when he saw how high he'd floated! "All right!" he cried. "Take whatever you want!"

On the ground below, Rachel and

Kirsty whooped and gave each other a high five.

Chelsea didn't waste a moment. In the blink of an eye, she flew up, plucked her magic balloon out of the bunch, and shrunk it down to fairy-size. She held tight to it with one hand while carefully using her wand to make a few of the goblin's other balloons disappear. As each balloon vanished, the goblin slowly lowered to the ground. When he landed on the pavement, he shouted with joy.

His friends weren't so happy, though.

"This is all your fault!" one hollered.

The other chimed in, "You ruined everything!"

Rachel couldn't listen to them bicker any longer. "You shouldn't have balloons at the zoo anyway," she said. "They're dangerous for the animals!"

The goblins looked sheepish. For once, they had nothing to say!

Chelsea swooped out of the sky and

flicked her wand. Fairy dust glimmered in the air. When it cleared, all of the goblins' balloons had vanished.

The goblins grumbled under their breaths and turned back to their empty cart. Together, they pushed it down the path. The girls could hear them muttering, "Pesky fairies ruin everything!" as they disappeared around a bend.

Chelsea gave Rachel and Kirsty each a kiss on the cheek. "I couldn't have done it without you, girls!" She tugged on the string of her magic balloon. "Now I need to get this back to Fairyland, so people everywhere can feel confident about trying new things."

Kirsty looked at her watch. "It's almost eleven o'clock already—time for the penguin feeding! I hope your balloon can help Clare with the penguins."

Chelsea winked. "You'd better hurry up. I think today's penguin feeding is going to be something you won't want to miss!"

And with that, she vanished in a swirl of sparkles.

Rachel grabbed Kirsty's hand. The two friends ran along the wooded pathways

until they came
to the penguin
exhibit. Mr.
and Mrs.
Walker waved
to them from a
spot in the
stands, and the
girls scurried
up the steps to
join them.

"You're just in time!"
Mrs. Walker said with a smile. "Did you
have fun exploring the zoo?"

"It was an adventure!" Rachel said.

Mr. Walker handed over two red
slushies in silly penguin cups. "We
thought you might be thirsty."

The girls' eyes lit up. They thanked

him and sipped their icy drinks as the announcer came over the loudspeaker.

"Ladies and gentlemen, boys and girls—welcome to Cove City Zoo's famous penguin feeding!"

The crowd cheered, but Rachel and Kirsty couldn't help feeling nervous as Clare stepped out onto a rock next to the water. She waved to the audience,

and the girls waved back, giving her thumbs-up. When Clare spotted them, her face lit up with a huge grin.

"She doesn't look worried anymore," Kirsty whispered.

Rachel chewed on her straw. "I hope the return of Chelsea's balloon has given Clare some confidence!"

As the feeding began, it was clear that Clare and the penguins were a perfect

team! The penguins performed every trick that Clare asked, happily gobbling up the fish that she offered them. The penguins splashed in the water, spun on the rocks, and made everyone laugh.

Rachel sighed in relief. "I think we found Chelsea's balloon just in time," she said. "Hopefully Ivy is feeling better about her graduation speech, too."

Kirsty cheered as one of the penguins slid across a rock on his belly. "I bet she is," she said. "And I bet her speech is going to be perfectly magical!"

Graduation
Celebration

Contents

Graduation Gone Bad

"What a beautiful spot for a graduation!" Kirsty said as she and Rachel walked into Cove City Park. The park was filled with leafy green trees, colorful flower beds, and sparkling fountains.

Rachel grinned. "It's hard to believe we're right in the middle of a city, isn't it?"

Up ahead,
Mr. and Mrs.
Walker walked
alongside
Ivy and her
parents.
"Come on,
girls!" Mr.
Walker called,
pointing to an
enormous lawn. "The
ceremony is this way!"

Rachel and Kirsty raced to catch up,
and they both gasped in awe as the lawn
spread out before them. Rows of white
folding chairs faced a huge stage. Just
beyond the stage was the glimmering
cove, which twinkled beautifully in the
afternoon sunlight.

"Ivy, this place looks perfect," Rachel said softly, squeezing her cousin's arm. "I'm so excited for your big day!"

Ivy smiled, straightening her cap and smoothing the wrinkles out of her long, black graduation gown. "Thanks! I have to go do a sound check so I know how to use the microphone when it's time for my speech. Wish me luck!"

The whole family hugged Ivy and waved as she headed to the stage.

"Well, girls," Mrs. Walker said, turning to Rachel and Kirsty, "the ceremony doesn't start for a while yet. The rest of the family will be here later. Do you two want to explore in the meantime? We'll save some seats."

"That sounds great!" Kirsty said. Once the adults had walked away, she turned to Rachel. "Do you want to check out the cove? It looks awfully magical . . ."

Rachel winked. "I sure hope it is!"

As the girls headed past the stage to the waterfront, they couldn't help noticing all sorts of commotion backstage. People seemed to be running around frantically.

A loud squeak rang through the air. "The speakers aren't working right!" someone cried.

"That's nothing," another voice chimed in. "We just found out that Principal

Doogan is stuck in traffic—and he has all of the diplomas in his car!"

Someone else piped up. "Has anyone seen the master list of graduates' names? It was right here, but now I can't find it anywhere!"

Rachel and Kirsty looked at each other in dismay. They knew exactly why everything was going wrong—and they were the only ones who could fix it!

"We have to find Chelsea's missing magic diploma," Rachel whispered urgently. "I don't even know

where to start
looking, though."

Kirsty sighed.
"Queen Titania
always says we
should let the
magic find
us . . . but we
don't have much
time. If we don't track
down the diploma soon, Ivy's graduation
ceremony will be an absolute disaster!"

Diploma Dilemma

Rachel and Kirsty left the chaotic stage behind and headed to the waterfront. The cove sparkled in the sunshine. It was so big that the girls could barely see where it opened up into the ocean!

"Look at all the boats out there," Rachel said, pointing at sailboats,

rowboats, kayaks, and motorboats
bobbing on the calm water.

Kirsty nodded. "And
so many people
are flying kites
on the beach!"
The colorful
kites sailed
overhead,
their tails
blowing in the
breeze. There
were kites in every
color of the rainbow!

As both girls peered up, Rachel
suddenly squeezed Kirsty's arm. "Did
you see that?"

"That kite is glimmering a little bit!"
Kirsty said excitedly, noticing a beautiful

purple kite with multicolored bows on its tail. She turned to Rachel, her eyes shining. "Do you think it could be . . . ?"

Just then, the kite dipped closer to the ground. The girls squinted to get a better look. Sure enough, they could see a tiny figure perched on the kite, her dark bangs blowing in the breeze.

"It's Chelsea!" Rachel cried.

Chelsea darted through the air so quickly that no one else was able to spot her. Rachel and Kirsty could hear her

laugh as she fluttered down and landed
lightly on Kirsty's shoulder.

"Hi, girls!" the little fairy called out
cheerfully, grinning up at them. "I'm so
happy to see you again."

"We're
happy
to see
you, too,
Chelsea,"
Kirsty
said, and
Rachel
used her

pinkie finger to give Chelsea a tiny
high five.

The girls made their way to a grassy
hill near the water, away from the
crowds. "I think we can talk here

without anyone seeing us," Rachel
noted. She plucked a fluffy dandelion
from the grass, and blew the seeds into
the air.

"Everyone in Fairyland was thrilled to
see my magic balloon," Chelsea
reported. "I can't thank you enough for
your help tracking it down!"

Kirsty frowned. "Things are still all
mixed-up here, I'm afraid," she said.

"Ivy's graduation starts soon, and nothing seems to be going right!" She blew on a dandelion with a frustrated huff.

Chelsea put her hands on her hips, looking determined. "We have to figure out what those terrible goblins have done with my magic diploma! Where should we start?"

Rachel and Kirsty both shrugged.

"I don't have a clue," Rachel said, staring down at her hands.

Kirsty nodded and lay back in the grass with a sigh. "Yeah, why bother? We'll never find your diploma in time to fix Ivy's graduation, anyway."

Chelsea
furrowed her
tiny eyebrows
and looked
at the girls
carefully.
Suddenly,
she snapped
her fingers.
"This is all
because of
my missing
diploma!" she

exclaimed. "It helps people be
persistent and see tasks through to
the end. Without it, you're both thinking
of giving up." She tugged on Kirsty's
braid with a twinkle in her eye. "But

that's why I need your help more than ever!"

Rachel and Kirsty both sat up straight, as though they'd been shocked out of their stupor. Chelsea was right!

Eye on the Prize

Before either Rachel or Kirsty could say anything, some noise out on the water caught their attention.

"What's going on out there?" Chelsea murmured, hovering above Rachel's head to get a better look.

The three friends could see a big green boat bobbing in the cove. A group of boys was yelling and laughing as they did cannonballs off the side of the boat into the water. Every time one of them landed, they splashed people in kayaks and canoes all around.

"How rude!" Kirsty said indignantly.

Rachel shook her head. "Why would anyone act like that?"

At that, Chelsea gasped and did an

excited tumble in the air. "Not why, WHO!" she said with a wink.

"Goblins!" Rachel and Kirsty cried together, their faces lighting up.

The boat was too far away to see if the boys really were goblins or not, but as the girls looked more closely, they noticed a huge flag fluttering off the stern of the boat. It was green . . . and had a picture of a giant, sneering goblin face on it!

Kirsty pointed out the flag to Chelsea. "That boat out there definitely belongs to the goblins!"

"I'll bet they have my magic diploma," Chelsea said with a grin. "It's so close, I can feel it!"

Rachel stared out at the water, thinking. "But how can Kirsty and I get out there?" she wondered. "We don't have a boat, and it's too far to swim."

The friends were silent for a moment. Then Chelsea clapped her hands in delight. "I have the perfect solution—I'll turn you both into fairies! Then we can all fly out to the boat together."

"Ooh, I love being a fairy!" Rachel said with a happy sigh.

"Me, too," Kirsty added. "Let's do it!"

With no time to waste, Chelsea murmured a spell under her breath and waved her wand. A shower of purple sparkles rained down on the girls. Before they knew it, they were the same size as Chelsea—and they had lovely, shimmery wings on their backs!

Kirsty fluttered her wings and smiled as she rose into the air. "This is the best feeling in the world," she said. "Come on, let's go!"

Rachel and Chelsea zipped up behind her as Kirsty darted out across the water. In no time at all, they reached the goblins' boat. Silently, they landed near the stern of the boat and hid behind the flapping goblin flag.

Luckily, the goblins were too busy causing chaos to notice them! But before long,

the green troublemakers climbed out
of the water and lounged
lazily in the sun.

One big-nosed
goblin yawned.
"This is the
life!" He sighed
contentedly.
"We should do
this more often."

A goblin in a
baseball cap
nodded in agreement.
"Here, it's just us. We don't have to
worry about anyone stealing the magic
diploma. We can just relax all day and
enjoy ourselves!"

Rachel, Kirsty, and Chelsea all looked
at one another and smiled. Not only did

the goblins definitely have Chelsea's magic diploma—but they were also about to get some surprise visitors!

But where was the diploma? Was it in a goblin's pocket? Hidden down below the boat deck? It could be anywhere! The fairies scanned the deck frantically, looking for a telltale sparkle.

Suddenly, Kirsty giggled. "Look!" she whispered, pointing to a goblin leaning over the side of the boat. He was peering out to sea through a telescope.

"Wait a minute," Rachel said, catching on. "That's not a telescope at all . . . he's looking through your magic diploma, Chelsea!"

Diploma Dodge

Rachel, Kirsty, and Chelsea watched the goblin carefully. Whispering, they came up with a plan to get the diploma back. It was risky, but they had to try!

The three friends took to the air and silently fluttered down near the goblin, who was still peering at the horizon through the diploma. On Chelsea's sign,

all three fairies suddenly began to fly
faster and faster! They zipped around the
goblin's head, wings buzzing.

"*Argh!*" the goblin cried frantically,
swatting them away. "I hate bugs!
Shoo! Shoo!"

Their plan was working—the goblin
thought they were bees or flies. They
were moving so fast, he had no idea that
he was surrounded by fairies!

There was no time to celebrate, though. Rachel, Kirsty, and Chelsea had to keep ducking, dodging, and swooping as the goblin flapped his hands and tried to knock them away.

Kirsty dipped under the goblin's flailing hand just in time, zooming up around his big ears. *Whew!*

Seconds later, Chelsea almost crashed into the goblin's nose when he unexpectedly turned his head! At the last minute, she did a spectacular tumble in the air, up and over his nose. That was close!

"Whoa!" Rachel cried as the goblin made contact with one of her wings and sent her spiraling out over the side of the boat. For a second, she was totally out of control! Was she going to crash right into the water?

Flapping her wings as hard as she could, Rachel righted herself and sailed upward. Not a moment too soon, her toes skimmed the surface of the water as she zoomed into the sky. If she hadn't regained control, her wings would have gotten wet, and she wouldn't have been able to fly at all! Rachel took a deep breath and rejoined her friends.

The goblin continued to dance around and swat the air. Nearby, his friends watched from their lounge chairs, laughing at him.

"Are you scared of a little bee?" one called out.

Another chuckled. "It looks like you're no match for those tiny bugs!"

The goblin flailed wildly, getting more and more frustrated. Finally, he swatted the air so hard that he flung the magic diploma right out of his hand. It went flying overboard!

"Oh, no! It's going to land in the water!" Kirsty cried.

Chelsea darted through the air like a streak of light. "Not if I can help it!" She used her powerful wings to swoop down and scoop up the diploma just before it splashed into the water. As her little hand touched it, the diploma shrank to fairy-size. It was safe at last!

Once Chelsea had the diploma, Rachel and Kirsty pulled up short and hovered above the goblin's head, breathing heavily. They were exhausted!

The goblin's eyes widened when he realized what had happened. He groaned and shook his fist at the girls. "You pesky fairies again!"

The other goblins weren't laughing anymore. In fact, they looked angry! They joined their friend at the railing, peering up at Rachel, Kirsty, and Chelsea.

"Why can't you just leave us alone?" one whined.

Another goblin stomped in frustration. "You're always getting us in trouble with Jack Frost!"

Rachel looked at them pointedly. "YOU'RE always taking things that

don't belong to
you. That's not
right!"

The goblins
all looked
down and
scuffed their
big feet. They
were silent for a
moment, before one mumbled, "Jack
Frost is mad at us, anyway. This is just
going to make it worse."

Kirsty couldn't help feeling a little sorry
for the goblins. "Why is he angry with
you?" she asked, perching on the railing.

"He just graduated from his master
class in Ice Magic," explained the goblin
who'd dropped the diploma. "We all
kind of forgot to congratulate him."

Another goblin looked sad. "We didn't mean to! But he decided that if he wasn't going to be congratulated for a job well done, no one would. That's why he stole your magic objects," he finished, looking at Chelsea and her little diploma with a shrug.

Chelsea crossed her arms. "Well, I can't give you the diploma back," she said. "It's not fair for Jack Frost to ruin everyone's special days."

"But maybe we can help you cheer him up!" Rachel said suddenly. She grinned. "Why don't you throw Jack Frost a surprise party at his Ice Castle?"

Kirsty smiled at her best friend. "That's a great idea, Rachel! I bet he'll be so thrilled about the party that he won't even be mad that you lost the magic diploma," she told the goblins.

The goblins began to dance around the boat deck. "I have to admit, you little fairies have some really big ideas!" one of them exclaimed.

"We just have to decide on a theme," the big-nosed goblin said. "How about an icy luau?"

The goblin in the baseball cap rolled his eyes. "That's a terrible idea! It should clearly be a frosty pirate-themed party."

The rest of the
goblins all groaned
and began yelling
at once.

Chelsea put
an arm around
each of the girls
and giggled.
"Typical!" she said.
"Come on, let's get
back to the park."

With Chelsea in the lead,
the three friends darted over the
glittering water, leaving the boat full of
squabbling goblins behind.

A Frosty Finish

The fairy friends reached the shore and flitted down to land behind a tree, out of sight. There, Chelsea gave Rachel and Kirsty each a big hug. Then she turned them back to their normal size with a quick flick of her wand.

"Congratulations, girls!" Chelsea cried, hovering in the air before them and

squeezing her
diploma to
her chest. "You
did it! I can't
thank you
enough for all
your help."
With a wave, she
disappeared in a
swirl of glittery fairy magic.

Rachel put an arm around Kirsty's
shoulders. "Another magical mission
complete!" she declared.

But before Kirsty could reply, a big
gust of chilly wind blew in from the
cove. Both girls shivered! They watched
as boats teetered precariously on the
water, kites broke from their strings, and
the grass took on an icy sheen.

"I don't like the looks of this," Kirsty said through chattering teeth.

A bolt of lightning crashed out of the sky and landed in a stand of trees nearby, making everyone on the beach scatter in fear. Rachel and Kirsty ducked behind a bench, but they knew that it wasn't real lightning. It was a bolt of ice lightning—and it was carrying Jack Frost!

"Come on," Rachel said, heading for the trees. "We need to get Jack Frost back to Fairyland before he ruins Ivy's graduation—or worse, before anyone spots him!"

The girls sprinted past the trees . . . and came face-to-face with Jack Frost. They'd met him many times before, of course, but his icy sneer was always shocking!

"What are you doing here?" Kirsty demanded, crossing her arms.

Jack Frost whirled to face her, scowling. "None of your business! I don't have to tell you pesky girls anything."

Rachel stepped forward. "We heard that you graduated from your master class in Ice Magic," she said gently. "That's really impressive!"

"Yeah, well, you're the only one who thinks so," Jack Frost huffed, his face softening a little. "No one even bothered to congratulate me. So even though that horrible fairy tricked my goblins into giving back her magic object, I'm here to make sure that this graduation is ruined!" He frowned.

"If you want something done right, I guess you just have to do it yourself."

Kirsty and Rachel exchanged glances.

"You know," Kirsty said carefully, "the goblins were just telling us that they were awfully proud of you." She lowered her voice to a whisper. "We're not supposed to say anything, but I think they were hoping to celebrate with you at the Ice Castle later today."

Jack Frost's eyes grew very wide. "Celebrate? Like a . . . party?" he said slowly.

"I think they wanted you to be really surprised, which is why they waited to throw the party until today," Rachel explained carefully.

A huge smile covered Jack Frost's icy face. He threw his hands in the air. "Of course! That makes perfect sense! I should have known! After all, it takes a while to plan a big, important bash."

Kirsty glanced down at her watch. "Exactly! I just hope you don't miss it . . ."

Jack Frost gasped. "They can't start without the guest of honor! I have to

go!" He disappeared in a burst of chilly air and swirling snowflakes.

Rachel flopped down on the ground. "That was close!"

"You're telling me," Kirsty said with a relieved sigh. "Now we need to get back—Ivy's graduation is about to start!"

Rachel jumped to her feet, and together the girls ran to the main lawn of the park. They quickly found Rachel's parents and took their seats just as music began to play. To their relief, everything seemed to be in place! The speakers were working, Principal Doogan had arrived with the diplomas, and the list of the graduates' names was up on the podium where it belonged.

The girls caught their breath as they watched the graduates file down the

aisle, wearing caps and gowns. When Ivy walked by, she waved and gave her family a huge smile. Rachel and Kirsty couldn't help cheering!

"I can't wait to hear Ivy's big speech and see her collect her diploma," Rachel whispered.

Kirsty squeezed her best friend's hand. "We know she's going to do great, thanks to Chelsea!"

THE BABY ANIMAL RESCUE FAIRIES

Don't miss any of Rachel and Kirsty's
other fairy adventures!
Check out this magical sneak peek of

Mae
the Panda Fairy!

A Visitor from Fairyland

Kirsty Tate gazed happily at the rows of bushes, her bare arm resting on the open window as the car traveled along the bumpy country road. Pretty red, yellow, and pink flowers were tangled among the green leaves. She could smell the tangy aroma of cut grass and the earthiness of freshly turned soil.

"We're almost there, girls," said Mrs. Tate from the driver's seat. "Look!"

She slowed the car and pointed at a sign at the side of the winding road.

2 MILES—WILD WOODS NATURE RESERVE

Kirsty smiled at her best friend, Rachel Walker, who was sitting beside her.

"I'm so excited," said Rachel. "The sun's shining, we've got the whole summer vacation stretched out ahead of us, and a whole week to spend here at the reserve with the animals."

It was the start of summer vacation, and Kirsty and Rachel were on their way to Wild Woods, their local nature reserve. Rachel was staying with Kirsty, and their parents had arranged for them to spend every day that week at the reserve as volunteers. As the car turned up a rough, narrow road, their hearts raced with anticipation.

"I can't wait to help out as a junior ranger," said Kirsty.

"It will be so cool to see the animals!"

At the end of the road was an archway, printed with green words:

WELCOME TO WILD WOODS
NATURE RESERVE

Mrs. Tate drove through the archway and stopped the car next to a small wooden hut. The door of the hut opened and a tan woman with dark brown hair came out. She was wearing khaki shorts, a white shirt, and hiking boots. She waved at them and smiled.

"Look, there's Becky," said Mrs. Tate. "She's the head of Wild Woods."

Rachel and Kirsty jumped out of the car, and Becky walked over to them.

"It's great to see you," said Becky, shaking their hands. "I'm really glad that you'll be spending the week with us. It's great to meet young people who are interested in conservation."

"We can't wait to get started!" said Rachel excitedly.

"I thought you could begin by exploring the reserve on your own a little," said Becky. "It's the best way to get a feel for it. I'll meet you back here this afternoon and give you your first task."

"That sounds great!" Kirsty cheered.

"A real adventure!" Rachel added.

"These two love adventures!" said Mrs. Tate with a laugh.

They grabbed their backpacks and some supplies for the day.

"Do you have everything?" asked Mrs. Tate kindly.

Kirsty peered into her backpack. "Camera, notebook, raincoat, pens, binoculars, sunscreen . . ." She grinned at her mother. "Yes, I think I've remembered everything!"

Mrs. Tate kissed her and gave Kirsty a hug. "Have a fantastic time," she said.

Rachel and Kirsty waved good-bye and hurried down a winding path into the reserve. As soon as they were out of sight, Kirsty paused and took a deep breath of fresh air. "I feel as if there's no one else for miles and miles," she said.

"It's wonderful!" Rachel smiled,

turning around slowly on the spot. "I can see dragonflies, bumblebees, and even a kingfisher!"

They were standing beside a large pond, which was surrounded by catttails. Everywhere they looked, they saw animals. Hares peeked at them, ducks paddled nearby, and otters slipped into the water. Kirsty fumbled in her backpack and pulled out her camera.

"This place is incredible," she said, taking picture after picture.

"Look over there," said Rachel, pulling out her camera, too. "The frog on that lily pad looks just like my stuffed animal at home."

"He does look familiar," Kirsty agreed, looking through her camera lens and zooming in. "Hang on—that's no ordinary frog! It's Bertram!"

Their friend, a royal frog footman from Fairyland, waved and came hopping over to them. Rachel and Kirsty knelt down beside the edge of the pond and smiled at him.

"Hello, Rachel and Kirsty!" he said in a surprised voice. "I didn't expect to meet you two here!"

"We didn't expect to see you, either," said Rachel with a giggle.

RAINBOW magic ™

Which Magical Fairies Have You Met?

- ❑ The Rainbow Fairies
- ❑ The Weather Fairies
- ❑ The Jewel Fairies
- ❑ The Pet Fairies
- ❑ The Dance Fairies
- ❑ The Music Fairies
- ❑ The Sports Fairies
- ❑ The Party Fairies
- ❑ The Ocean Fairies
- ❑ The Night Fairies
- ❑ The Magical Animal Fairies
- ❑ The Princess Fairies
- ❑ The Superstar Fairies
- ❑ The Fashion Fairies
- ❑ The Sugar & Spice Fairies
- ❑ The Earth Fairies
- ❑ The Magical Crafts Fairies

■ SCHOLASTIC

Find all of your favorite fairy friends at
scholastic.com/rainbowmagic

HiT entertainment

RMFAIRY11